To Beth

Houghton Mifflin Books for Children is an imprint of
Houghton Mifflin Harcourt Publishing Company.

www.hmhbooks.com

The text of this book is set in Gararond.
The illustrations are acrylics on illustration board.

Library of Congress Cataloging-in-Publication Data
Hassett, Ann (Ann M.).
Too many frogs / by Ann and John Hassett.
p. cm.
Summary: With rapidly increasing numbers of frogs coming out of her basement,
Nana Quimby asks assorted neighborhood children for help, but finally it is up to her
to come up with a solution.
ISBN 978-0-547-36299-1
[1. Frogs—Fiction.] I. Hassett, John. II. Title.
PZ7.H2784Too 2011   [E]—dc22   2010006783

Manufactured in China
LEO 10 9 8 7 6 5 4 3 2 1
4500276009

TOO MANY FROGS!

by Ann and John Hassett

Houghton Mifflin Books for Children

Houghton Mifflin Harcourt

Boston   New York   2011

Nana Quimby was making a cake. She heard a damp sort of sound at her cellar door. She opened the door and found the cellar filled with water. Nana Quimby rushed to the window. "Too much water," she cried.

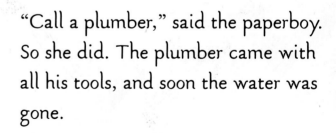

"Call a plumber," said the paperboy. So she did. The plumber came with all his tools, and soon the water was gone.

Nana Quimby stirred the cake batter. She heard a *thump* at the cellar door. She opened the door, and ten frogs hopped across the kitchen floor.

Nana Quimby rushed to the window. "Too many frogs," she cried. "Put the frogs in a goldfish bowl," said a girl jumping up and down. So she did.

Nana Quimby poured the batter into the pan. She heard a *thump-thump* at her cellar door. She opened the door, and twenty frogs hopped across the kitchen floor.

Nana Quimby rushed to the window.
"Too many frogs," she cried.
A boy running fast said,
"Put the frogs in cups of water."

So she did.

Nana Quimby put the cake into the oven.
She heard a *thump-thump-bang* at her
cellar door. She opened the door, and thirty
frogs hopped across the kitchen floor.

Nana Quimby rushed to the window.
"Too many frogs," she cried.
A girl tossing a stick said,
"Put the frogs in pots and pans."

So she did.

Nana Quimby washed the bowls. She heard a *thump-thump-bang-bang* at her cellar door. She opened the door, and forty frogs hopped across the kitchen floor.

Nana Quimby rushed to the window.
"Too many frogs," she cried.
A boy with a cat said,
"Put the frogs in the sink."

So she did.

Nana Quimby took the cake out of the oven.
She heard a *thump-thump-bang-bang-bonk*
at the cellar door. She opened the door, and
fifty frogs hopped across the kitchen floor.

Nana Quimby rushed to the window.
"Too many frogs," she cried.
A girl with a bat said,
"Put the frogs in the washing machine."

So she did.

Nana Quimby set the cake to cool. She heard a *thump-thump-bang-bang-bonk-bonk* at the cellar door. She opened the door, and one hundred frogs hopped across the kitchen floor.

Nana Quimby rushed to the window.
"Too many frogs," she cried.
A boy with a bicycle said,
"Put the frogs in the bathtub."

So she did.

Nana Quimby frosted the cake. She heard
a *thump-thump-bang-bang-bonk-bonk-
boom* at the cellar door. She opened the door,
and a million frogs hopped, jumped, bumped,
and bounced across the kitchen floor.

Nana Quimby rushed to the window.
"Too many frogs," she cried.
But there was no one to answer . . .

She scratched her head, then said,
"Put the frogs in the cellar and fill
it full of water."

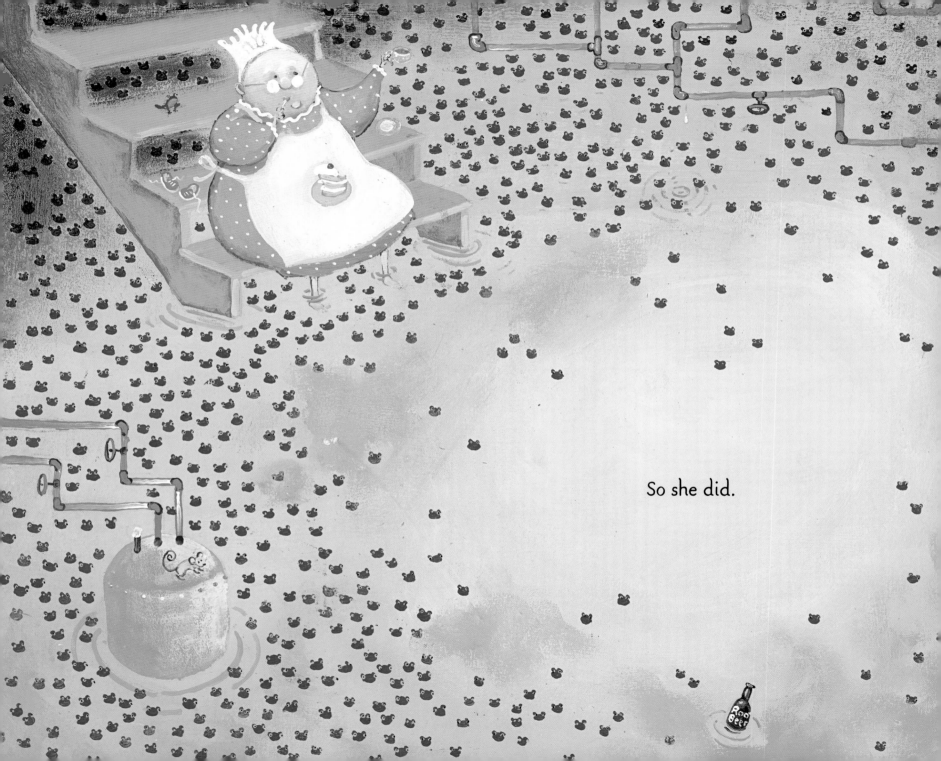

So she did.